spine
chillers

spine chillers

stories chosen by
wendy cooling

Dolphin

A Dolphin Paperback

First published in Great Britain in 1997
by Orion Children's Books
a division of the Orion Publishing Group Ltd
Orion House
5 Upper St Martin's Lane
London WC2H 9EA

A catalogue record for this book is available
from the British Library
Typeset by Deltatype Ltd, Birkenhead, Merseyside
Printed in Great Britain by Clays Ltd, St Ives plc
ISBN 1 85881 454 5

contents

beads in a hollow

hazel townson

The house had a secret, but Jim Archer did not tell his son in case it put young Sam off wanting to live there. Besides, he told himself, every old house must have a secret of some sort or another, and this was a fine, well-constructed building on offer at a bargain price. It had an extensive garden, too. Sam could take the garden over as his personal playground. One of his constant complaints was lack of space, so he'd be thrilled with this.

And indeed, Sam Archer took to that garden in a big way. He had never had such a huge area to himself before. It was full of possibilities and became his secret kingdom. All through that first long summer holiday he spent every waking minute in the garden, playing and planning and weaving his fantasy world.

Then one day a girl appeared, leaning over the gate, staring into Sam's garden. She wasn't bad-looking, Sam had to admit, with her fair hair falling almost to her waist. A bit like Alice in Wonderland. But she had no business to be there.

Sam Archer scowled. 'What do you want?'

'Just looking.'

'Well, go and look somewhere else,' he snapped rudely.

The girl was a fraction taller than Sam, but about the same age, he guessed. Her steady gaze made him feel uncomfortable. He was supposed to be tough. Girls usually looked away when he scowled at them.

'I used to live here,' said the girl.

Sam's lip curled. 'Oh, yeah?'

He knew very well that she was telling lies.

'That was my bedroom window, up there.'

She was pointing to Sam's room.

'You're just snooping around. Well, let me tell you I don't like nosy parkers.'

'I wanted to see the house again, that's all. For old times' sake. Only the outside. I promise I won't intrude. Do you mind if I just come into the garden?'

Sam was amazed at her cheek. 'Yes, I do mind! This is private property. Get lost!'

The girl gave him a tight little smile which did not reach her eyes, and which Sam did not like at all.

'You're not very polite, are you?' she complained. 'In fact, I'd say you were rude. And that's a pity, because I wanted to ask you a favour.'

She leaned further over the gate and stared intently at Sam.

I suppose she thinks a stare like that could hypnotise me into doing what she wants, Sam thought. How dare she?

'I don't do favours,' he declared, then deliberately turned his back on her and began marching possessively over his territory towards the house.

The garden was his; nobody else's. It was a good place to play because his dad didn't care about it. If his mother had still been with them she would have planted it with all kinds of flowers and shrubs, but his dad had more important things to do. Apart from the trees, long, tangled grass and weeds were the only things that grew there. It was Sam's very own secret place and nobody was going to come barging in, especially not a stranger, and a girl at that.

Anyway, she was lying. She had never lived here; it was just an excuse to worm her way in. Sam remembered Mrs Foster, the elderly widow who had sold them the house. Mrs Foster had explained that she had been born there and had lived in the house for all of her eighty years. She

....

had never had any children. So how could this girl be telling the truth?

When Sam had almost reached the house the girl called after him: 'Did you find the hollow at the top of the oak tree?'

Sam paused, pretending to tie his shoelace, but he kept his back to her. He did not want her to guess that he was listening.

'That was my special secret hiding place,' the girl went on. 'The last things I hid in there were some blue and green beads, but I had to go away suddenly so I wasn't able to collect them. They should still be up there, unless the magpies have found them. The favour I was going to ask you was whether I could come in and rescue the beads. But if you won't let me into the garden, perhaps you would fetch the beads down for me yourself? I'd be ever so grateful.'

Hidden beads! A likely story!

Sam did not even think it worth a reply. He stamped into the house and slammed the door. When he looked out of the kitchen window a few minutes later, the girl had gone.

After lunch, Sam wandered back into the garden. First he made sure the girl was nowhere to be seen. Then he began to climb the oak tree.

He told himself he would have climbed it anyway, whether the girl had mentioned it or not. If there really was a hollow up there, it would make a brilliant hiding-place. Just what he needed!

Sam's favourite tree was the sycamore in the west corner, which he was gradually transforming into a treehouse. That took up most of his time, so he hadn't paid much attention to the oak. Perhaps it was high time he did, then, girl or no girl.

He could see that the oak would be much harder to climb than the sycamore. It reached much higher and there were far fewer decent footholds. In fact, Sam's dad had advised him never to climb it. (Not that that mattered for he did not take advice from anybody. Sam Archer was perfectly capable of making his own decisions.) Anyway, it was a challenge, and he liked challenges.

He went into the house and fetched a rucksack which he slung across his shoulders. He put some biscuits in it, so as not to admit to himself that the rucksack was really intended as a container for the beads. There weren't any beads. The whole thing was just a rather childish send-up.

It proved a tiring climb. Sam had to rest halfway up, then again, and again. It was the most difficult climb he had ever tackled. Where there might have been likely footholds some of the branches had been chopped away. Yet though he had to concentrate hard, he still examined carefully every metre of that tree. It was as solid as a ship's mast; no hollows anywhere. Well, he had known perfectly well that the girl was just a mischief-maker, of course. But there might still have been a hollow in the tree, just by coincidence. He could not help feeling disappointed.

Then, when he was nearly at the top, he suddenly spotted the hollow, just about where she had said it would be. Now he felt excited. Carefully he shuffled along a not-too-sturdy branch and stretched his arm forward to explore inside the hollow.

Watch out! Mustn't lean too far!

There was a space just big enough for his hand, and almost at once his fingers closed over something knobbly and hard. Swaying precariously on his branch, he managed to draw out a filthy string of beads covered in the dust of long-dead leaves.

When he had blown away the dust and rubbed the beads up on his tee-shirt he found they were made of blue and green glass. Blue and green, exactly as the girl had said.

Had she been telling the truth after all? Or had she just happened to see someone else put them there?

Well, he certainly wasn't going to give her the beads. They were in his tree, in his garden, so they were *his* beads now.

Slowly, Sam transferred the beads to the rucksack and was just fastening it when his dad came round the corner.

Jim Archer heard a rustling noise, looked up, and could scarcely believe what he saw. He had forbidden Sam ever to climb the oak tree and was thoroughly alarmed to see his son in such a dangerous position. He called out a warning:

'Sam! Don't move! Don't try to climb down by yourself; stay right where you are. Just hang on for a couple of minutes and I'll go and fetch the ladder. Hold on tight now, son; I won't be long.'

At the sound of his dad's voice Sam made the mistake of looking down.

It seemed a long way to the ground. He hadn't realised how far he had climbed. His stomach lurched and he began to feel dizzy. The trees about him began to shift and spin like a merry-go-round. Sam wanted to shout but found that he couldn't. His voice didn't seem to work. Cold sweat broke out on his forehead and his limbs began to shake.

So – he wasn't as macho as he had always imagined. Sam no longer cared about the humiliation of having to be rescued. He just closed his eyes and prayed: 'Hurry up with that ladder, Dad!'

Then something even worse happened. He opened his

eyes again and spotted the girl's face grinning up at him. She was standing near the sycamore. Where on earth had she sprung from? And how dare she come into his garden after all he'd said? Well, he must certainly not let her see how scared he was.

Suddenly the girl reached up her cupped hands to him, as if asking him to drop the beads down into them ... and as Sam stared in amazement he could have sworn that those hands passed right through the trunk of the sycamore! They couldn't have, of course. Fear must be making him hallucinate. Now the whole world rocked and reeled. Sam lost his grip on the branch and fell crashing to the ground, just as his father came hurrying round the corner with the ladder.

Jim Archer saw no girl in the garden, nor did he find anything but a packet of crushed biscuits and a handful of dust in his dead son's haversack.

For the rest of his life the poor man blamed himself for startling Sam and causing him to fall from the oak tree and break his neck – exactly as Mrs Foster's younger sister had done nearly eighty years before.

the ghost
on the track

roger stevens

Bruno dropped the ball at Dan's feet. Dan picked it up. 'Good boy,' he said and threw it high over the wooden fence at the bottom of the garden. It bounced across the sunny field of golden stubble. With a yelp of pleasure, Bruno went bounding after it.

Dan's mum came out of the cottage door. She had her sun hat on and a big shopping basket in her hand.

'Don't lose that ball,' she said.

'I won't,' Dan replied.

'I won't be long. Are you sure you'll be okay?' his mum asked.

'Of course I will.'

'Well, don't go wandering too far from the cottage.'

'Of course I won't,' Dan said. He watched her walk around the cottage to the front gate.

'Don't forget the pizza,' Dan called after her.

'Don't worry, I won't,' she called back as she got into the car. The noise of the car's engine faded away and Dan listened to the sounds of the countryside. Birds sang, insects chirruped and bees buzzed. But best of all, you couldn't hear the noise of traffic.

Bruno bounded back with the ball.

'That's enough,' Dan said. 'We're going to explore.'

It wasn't the holiday Dan wanted. He would have liked to go to the seaside or Disneyland. But his dad had left them and his mum had wanted to go somewhere quiet and peaceful to think. It was certainly quiet here. The cottage was in the middle of nowhere. But the sun was blazing down and Dan had decided to make the most of it.

He went through the garden gate. It was only the beginning of August but the wheat had already been harvested. A footpath ran along the edge of the field and disappeared into some trees. Dan, with Bruno at his heels, followed it.

Once through the trees the path began to climb. Ahead of them was a huge hill. They made slow progress and by the time they reached the top, Dan was hot and thirsty.

'I should have brought some Coke,' he told Bruno.

The view was fantastic. Dan could see for miles in every direction. Behind him he could see their cottage and the road that led to the village where his mum had gone shopping. Directly below, in the valley, there was a railway line and a station. It looked deserted. A small road, with high hedges, ran from the station and disappeared around the hill.

Dan remembered what his mum had said. *Don't go wandering too far from the cottage.* But it wasn't far. It wouldn't take long. 'Come on. Let's take a look,' Dan said to the dog.

As they clambered down the steep footpath Dan could see that the railway only had a single track. He approached the station slowly, afraid that he might be trespassing. Any moment someone might appear and tell him off. But there was no sign of anyone.

Dan reached the railway and peered along it. Ahead the track disappeared into a tunnel. Behind him it curved around the side of the hill. There was no sign of any trains. The rails were rusted and brown weeds and blue forget-me-nots grew from the gravel. He climbed the edge of the platform and looked around. The sign said Topham Halt. The paint was peeling and ivy was creeping up around it.

'Anybody at home?' Dan yelled.

Bruno was running backwards and forwards along the track, trying to find a way up onto the platform.

'This way, Bruno,' he called, and ran along the platform.

Bruno barked and ran along below him. The end of the platform sloped down and the dog ran to join him, panting. An old-fashioned signal stood at the end of the platform. Dan had signals like that in the train set his dad had given him. The signal had a narrow wooden arm, like a red and white flag, which stuck out across the track and meant stop.

'I wonder how long it is since trains ran here?' Dan asked Bruno.

There was a loud click and the signal's arm went up, making Dan jump. He looked around, wondering if he'd knocked a lever or something.

'Hello, there,' a voice called. Dan spun round in surprise. They weren't alone after all.

2

'You'll be wanting a ride on the Topham Flyer,' the man said.

'Who are you?' Dan asked.

'I'm the stationmaster,' the man said, smiling. 'You can call me Bill if you like. Is this your dog?'

Dan nodded.

'Then I suppose you'll want a ticket for him as well.'

'No, I'm sorry,' Dan said. 'I don't want to go anywhere.'

'What are you doing here, then?' Bill asked. 'Are you meeting someone off the train?'

'Er, no,' Dan said. 'I was just looking around. I'm on

holiday. We're staying at the cottage over the hill. I thought the station was deserted.'

The stationmaster laughed. 'Goodness me, no. We run a regular service here. There are two trains every day. One goes east and the other goes west. Are you sure you don't want a ticket? You could get off at the next stop. Little Greening is only a mile down the track. If you got off there you'd just catch the next train coming back.'

Dan thought about this. It would be exciting. He had only been on a train once before, and that was to London. They went everywhere by car.

'How much is the fare?' Dan asked.

'How much have you got?'

Dan felt in his pocket and pulled out a pound coin. He'd been saving it for an ice cream.

'I've got a pound,' Dan said.

'That's exactly the fare.' The man reached in the top pocket of his uniform and pulled out a ticket. Then from another pocket he produced a small silver pair of clippers. He clipped the ticket and handed it to Dan. 'That'll be one pound, please,' he said.

Dan handed over his pound coin and took the ticket. It was a small piece of yellow card with *Little Greening : Return* written on it.

Bill was studying the coin. 'I've never seen one of these before,' he said. 'This *is* a real pound, is it? You're not trying to pull a fast one on me, are you, young man?'

'No, it's a pound,' Dan said, puzzled.

'It must be a new thing,' the stationmaster said. 'Well, I'll take your word for it. It takes a while for new inventions like this to reach these parts.' He slipped the coin in his pocket.

'What about Bruno?' Dan asked.

'Bruno?'

'My dog.'

'Ah,' Bill said and laughed. 'Tell you what. He can go free. How's that?'

'Thanks,' Dan said.

There was a loud whistle. It startled a group of black crows who had been squabbling over the remains of a dead rabbit by the track. They rose into the air with a screech and clatter of wings.

Bill pulled out a pocket watch and looked at it. 'That's the Topham Flyer,' he said. 'Right on time.'

A plume of white smoke rose over the hill. The rails began to hum. The train appeared and Dan gasped in surprise. The Topham Flyer was a steam engine.

The locomotive gleamed in the sun. It pulled three carriages, painted brown and cream. With a clanking of pistons, and a great sigh of steam, the train pulled slowly into the station and lurched to a stop. Nobody got off.

'It's never very busy on a Monday,' Bill said. 'There'll be plenty of people getting on at Little Greening though. They'll be going into town for the market.'

Dan followed Bill along the platform to the middle carriage.

'Enjoy your trip,' Bill said, as Dan opened the door.

'I will, and thanks.'

Bruno looked at the open door and growled suspiciously.

'It's only a train,' Dan told the dog. 'Don't be scared. Come on, it won't hurt you.'

Bruno growled again but followed Dan reluctantly into the carriage.

'Come and see me again,' Bill said. 'We can have a chat. It gets lonely out here sometimes.'

'I will,' Dan promised. Bill slammed the door shut.

Then he looked both ways along the platform and produced a whistle. He winked at Dan and blew it.

The train whistled in reply. Then, with a shudder and a lurch, it began to move. Dan settled back into his seat and looked around. A corridor ran down the other side of the carriage. Opposite him, on the wall, was a framed picture of a Welsh castle. Bruno was sniffing at a stain on the seat opposite.

The train began to pick up speed. Dan looked out of the window. They were going into the tunnel. There was a clump and Dan's ears popped. Bruno barked and then everything went black.

Dan could just make out wisps of steam passing the window as his eyes got used to the darkness. Bruno gave a little whimper.

'Don't worry,' he whispered to the dog. 'It's just a tunnel. We'll be through it in a minute.' He reached down and stroked Bruno's head.

Dan was wondering why the lights hadn't come on, when the train left the tunnel and he was blinking in the bright sunshine.

Plumes of white steam drifted by. They were travelling quite fast now. The wheels made a clickety-clack noise on the rails. Dan peered out of the window at the trees and brambles gliding by. In the distance the hills hardly moved, while below him the shadow of the train raced over the weeds and grass that grew along the track.

A horse was pulling a cart across a field of stubble. The farmer was heaving a bale of hay on to the back of the cart with a pitchfork. He glanced up at the train. Dan waved.

'Look at that,' Dan said, amazed. 'They still use horses here.'

Now they were passing some cottages. He waved at a

....

woman hanging out washing. She waved back. A road ran along the edge of the railway and they overtook an old black car. The train blew its whistle and they flashed across a level crossing. There were more houses now.

'We must be coming into Little Greening,' Dan said. 'There must be two railway tracks here so that the trains can pass one another.'

He pulled the window down and stuck his head out. The breeze was lovely and cool after the stuffy carriage and he could see the station approaching.

But the train wasn't slowing down. The whistle blew again and the train clattered through the station. Dan caught a glimpse of the sign – Little Greening. Bill, the stationmaster, had said the train stopped there. But they weren't stopping. There were people on the platform but they passed in a blur.

In moments the train was through the station. Ahead, Dan could see the signal. It said stop. The train should have stopped at the station and now it had gone through a red signal. Dan sat back down on the seat, close to panic. What should he do?

He thought about his mum. She would be back with the pizzas soon. She would be worried. He should never have got on the train.

Then Dan remembered that trains had an emergency lever you could pull. He looked frantically around but he couldn't see one.

Bill had said that the trains passed at Little Greening. Dan rushed to the other window in the corridor. He could see that they were still on a single track. If the other train was coming towards them they would hit it.

Dan grabbed Bruno. 'Something's gone wrong,' he told the dog. 'What are we going to do? We're going to crash!'

3

'We must keep calm,' Dan told Bruno. But he didn't feel calm. 'There must be an explanation for this. Perhaps the stationmaster was wrong about the train stopping here. Perhaps he made a mistake.'

Perhaps someone else on the train will know where the train stops next, Dan thought. 'Come on,' he said to Bruno. 'Let's see if we can find someone.' He stepped into the corridor and Bruno followed him towards the back of the train. Every compartment was empty. The last carriage opened out into a large guard's room. There was nobody there.

'I wonder where the guard is?' Dan said. 'Let's try the front of the train.'

They made their way back along the swaying corridor to the front, but every compartment in the front was empty too.

'I don't believe it,' Dan said. 'We're the only ones on the train. This is weird.'

The corridor ended in a door. There was a small window in the door and Dan peered through it. He could see the back of a wagon piled high with coal and a metal ladder that ran to the top.

Dan crouched down and stroked Bruno's head. 'Bill said that the train stopped at Little Greening. It's a single track and the trains pass there, but we went through a red signal and didn't stop. So there's probably another train on a collision course with us right now. We're the only ones on the train and Mum will be worried sick. What are we going to do?'

Bruno licked Dan's face.

'I don't know, either,' Dan said.

Dan stood up and looked out at the countryside racing

....

by. Perhaps the driver's injured, he thought. What if we can't stop? That would explain why we went through the red signal. 'Maybe if I look over the top of the coal wagon I can see if the driver's all right.'

Bruno barked.

'You think I should, eh?' Dan said.

He peered through the small window at the metal ladder. Should he try and climb it? It looked dangerous as it swayed to and fro with the motion of the train. Well, it wouldn't hurt to try, would it? The train was slowing now, as it began to climb a hill.

Dan made up his mind. He would give it a go.

He opened the door. A blast of cold air rushed into the carriage.

'Stay here,' he shouted at Bruno above the noise of the engine, now huffing and puffing up the slope.

'Here goes,' he said, and grabbed the ladder. Climbing the swaying wagon proved easier than he thought and he was soon at the top. He could see the engine clearly over the top of the coal. It was very windy here and he held on tightly. Steam and specks of soot rushed past him.

Carefully he raised himself higher, still clutching the ladder tightly. On each side of him the ground fell away as the train pulled up the hill.

He could see the driver's cabin quite clearly through the gusts of steam and smoke. It was empty. The train had no driver. The train was out of control.

Dan was scared. Carefully he turned and looked back down at Bruno. What should he do? Should he climb over the coal to the engine? Perhaps he could stop the train. But he had no idea how a steam engine worked. He was pretty sure that you couldn't just turn a switch and turn the engine off.

He peered ahead. They were almost at the top of the hill

now. Up ahead the track curved to the right and on to a bridge. Dan gasped in fear and surprise. It was bad enough that the train had no driver. What he saw now terrified him.

There was something wrong with the bridge. Half of it was missing. The bridge and the railway track came to a sudden end halfway across. The train would hurtle off the end and plunge into the valley below. They would be killed!

4

Quickly, Dan clambered back down the ladder. The train was beginning to pick up speed again. They were nearly at the broken bridge. Dan leapt back into the carriage and slammed the door behind him. Bruno barked, his tail wagging, and jumped up at Dan.

'We'll have to jump,' Dan said urgently. 'Quickly!'

He tried to open the outside carriage door. It was jammed. Desperately Dan tugged at the handle. There was a loud rumbling noise as the heavy engine began to cross the bridge. He gave the door one huge shove and it sprang open. He pushed the dog out in front of him and leapt into space. He hit the ground with a thump and tumbled down the grassy hillside. Then everything blacked out.

Dan woke up to find Bruno licking his face. For a moment he had no idea where he was. Then he remembered the runaway train. He sat up and gazed around. Above him he could see the broken bridge, rising out of a lake. A lake? He didn't remember seeing the water there before, but everything had happened so quickly. There was no sign of

the train. It must have gone off the end and into the
water. At least there was no one else on board.

He pulled himself groggily to his feet, feeling bruised
and shaken. He had a grassy scrape along the side of his
arm but at least he hadn't broken any bones.

'Come on,' he said to Bruno. 'Let's go home. Mum will
be panicking and I'm hungry.'

Bruno barked and wagged his tail.

'Okay,' Dan smiled. 'I'll give you a piece of my pizza.'

At leat it would be easy to find their way home: all they
had to do was follow the railway line. Dan wondered what
he would say when they reached Little Greening station.
The station must have alerted the emergency services to
tell them about the runaway train. Any moment now he
expected to see a helicopter looking for the train. Surely
they knew that the bridge was down?

They began the long hike home.

It was easy going, all downhill. They followed the track
for about a quarter of an hour until it began a long, lazy
curve into a valley. They rounded the bend and Dan
stopped and stared in astonishment. The valley was
flooded. They were looking at a huge lake. All he could see
was miles and miles of water.

The railway track led to a concrete wall and then
stopped. Dan walked to the wall and looked down. There
below him was water and no sign of a railway.

'Well, Bruno,' he said. 'What do you make of that?'

It was late afternoon when Dan and Bruno finally reached
the cottage. Dan's feet ached. They'd followed a path
around the edge of the lake which had lasted for miles.
They also saw a sign which said *South Reservoir – Keep Out*,
but there was no sign of Little Greening. And all the time

Dan's tummy had been rumbling with hunger. All he'd been able to think about was pizza.

His mum rushed to greet him and hugged him. 'Where have you been? Where have you been?' she sobbed. 'I was so worried.'

'I thought he'd turn up safe,' a voice said.

Dan looked up. It was a policeman. 'You okay?' he said.

Dan nodded. 'I'm sorry,' he said. 'I expect you heard about the accident?'

'Accident? Oh no,' his mum said and hugged him again.

'I'm not surprised,' the policeman said. 'There are some mad drivers round these parts.'

'No, not a road accident,' Dan said. 'It was a train accident.'

'A train accident,' said the policeman, frowning. 'There's no railway here. They closed the branch line nearly thirty years ago.'

'But I was on the train,' Dan said. 'There was no driver. We went through Little Greening and then we reached a bridge. It was broken. The train went off the end and I jumped …'

'It's okay,' Dan's mum said and hugged him again.

The policeman looked up at the clear, blue sky. 'Reckon Dan's got a touch of the sun,' he said to his mum. 'He's got no hat.' He looked at Dan. 'You ought to wear a hat in this weather, you know.'

His mum nodded. 'Let's go inside,' she said. 'You look terrible. I bet you're thirsty. And hungry. I've got pizza indoors, ready to go in the oven. And a bone for you, Bruno.'

'That's right, get him into the shade,' the policeman said kindly. 'No, there's not been a railway here since they built the reservoir and flooded Little Greening.'

Dan stared at the policeman. What did he mean? Little Greening wasn't flooded. He'd seen it. 'What about the station at Topham?' he asked the policeman.

'Oh, you've seen the station have you?' the policeman said. 'Yes, that's still there. But there's been no trains for years. The station's derelict now.'

Dan's mum thanked the policeman.

'That's okay,' the policeman said. 'Enjoy your holiday.'

Dan followed his mum into the cottage. What did the policeman mean? How could Little Greening be flooded? He'd seen the village himself. He'd travelled through it. Or had he imagined it? Then he remembered the ticket. He put his hand in his pocket. There it was. He pulled it out – a small yellow card, with a hole where the stationmaster had clipped it. And on it was written *Little Greening : Return*.

The policeman watched them go into the cottage. He looked down at the dog. Bruno had a ball in his mouth. He dropped it at the policeman's feet and wagged his tail.

'I lived in Little Greening before it was flooded,' the policeman told the dog. 'I watched them build the bridge when I was a boy. Pity it never got finished. Well, that's progress, I suppose.'

He picked the ball up and threw it. Bruno bounded after it.

the grey pony

mal lewis jones

The galloping hooves woke her. Both her arms were pinned inside the tight bedcovers and for a few moments she had to struggle to get them free.

She got out of bed and peered from the hotel window, which overlooked the sea-front. The lights from the bars and late-opening shops streamed across the road and the concrete promenade which skirted it.

Charmaine guessed the tide was out; she would have seen reflections on the water if the sea had been up to the promenade. There was no light on the beach at all. And the beach, she was sure, was where the pony ran, its mane flying, its hooves pounding the sand.

She screwed up her eyes and peered as hard as she could over the promenade, but she could see nothing of the beach. It was as if the ordinary world ended at the promenade. Beyond that, everything was dark and mysterious.

Charmaine turned from the window and looked at the neatly furnished bedroom. She hated its rectangular teak furniture and clinically white walls and bedcover.

Her younger brother, Leon, was lying asleep in the twin bed, one brown arm crooked over his head, the other flung out on top of the pale coverlet. He looked even younger than his nine years at that moment. Cherubic, like a choir-boy should.

A stab of jealousy entered her heart. Leon had been singled out, in a way that Charmaine never had. He had gained a scholarship to the Hereford Cathedral School. Leon had the most amazing singing voice. A pure treble, which won the admiration of all who heard it.

All but Charmaine, that is. She resented his ability. She

had never excelled at anything. She was, as her mother often described her, 'a plodder'.

Quickly, she looked back out of the window. Thinking about Leon's success was painful.

As Charmaine stared into the void beyond the promenade, the sound of hooves reached her ears once more.

She shivered. For the last year or so, she had had a recurring dream about riding a pony on a beach. It was always the same pony – dappled grey, with a long wavy, tousled mane, and sea-green eyes. He was sleek and nimble and fast as the wind, with the beauty and grace of a totally wild animal.

Nothing like the heavy-footed nags she was fobbed off with at the riding school.

Charmaine had been going to riding lessons for three years now. Ever since she could remember, she had wanted to be a showjumper when she grew up. The lessons had enabled her to learn the basic skills of riding, and she always enjoyed them. But while a few of the other girls were promoted to the more advanced class, Charmaine stayed where she was, just plodding along.

'She'll never set the world alight!' Charmaine overheard her riding teacher tell her mother one Saturday. 'But she'll end up making a competent horse-woman.'

The memory stung her. Why shouldn't she set the world alight! But somehow, at the riding school, just like everywhere else, she never got the chance to shine.

In her dream, it was different. No saddle, no tack, no reins, no teachers. Just her, the grey pony and the sand.

Charmaine checked her watch. It was not all that late. Her parents would be down in the bar for at least another hour.

She would go down to the beach, to find the grey pony. Her pony. It would be just like her dream.

She would go down and stand on the beach, and the grey pony would come thudding along the sand and halt at her feet, neighing in welcome. She would mount him and ride on his back, with the salt wind in her hair.

Next would come the most incredible feeling of elation. No longer dumpy, ploddy Charmaine. But another Charmaine entirely. The Charmaine who was trapped inside her, who could only be free in her dream life.

And then … ? But she could never remember what happened at the end of the dream.

Pulling on leggings and a jumper over her pyjamas, she had a sudden thrill of fear. She would go down to the beach. But not alone.

Leon could come with her. She didn't really want him to see the pony, but she was scared to go alone. Charmaine could bully him into keeping quiet. That was one good thing about being the oldest. She could always run rings around him, even now he was at the Cathedral School, and had started putting on 'airs and graces'.

With the pony's hooves still pounding in her ears, she slipped into the en-suite bathroom.

As soon as she closed the door behind her, the sound was cut off. She experienced a moment of doubt. Perhaps she had been dreaming, all this time? She padded back to the door and opened it again.

There was the unmistakable sound of hooves once more, assailing her through the open window.

Decisive now, she shook Leon awake.

'Will you come to the beach with me?'

'Don't want to,' said Leon, closing his eyes again. 'Wanna sleep.'

She shook him again. 'Look, Leon, this is *really* important.'

'Gerroff, Charmaine,' he moaned.

She forced him to sit up. 'There's a pony out there. I can hear him. Listen!'

They sat without speaking for several seconds, but there was a sudden burst of traffic outside on the road. Charmaine grew impatient.

'I'm going down, whether you come or not.'

She stood up, defiant.

'Oh, I'll come,' said Leon, scrambling out of bed. 'But what's a pony doing on the beach at this time of night? Is someone riding him?'

'No-one's riding him,' said Charmaine. 'Not yet. Get dressed quickly!'

Leon grumbled, but did as he was told.

It was easy enough moving through the hotel without attracting attention – there were still plenty of kids about at that time of night. Charmaine and Leon's parents were strict about bedtime. They were always sent up to their room hours before the other children in the hotel.

Crossing the road was trickier. They were exposed to the bar windows, which fronted the street. Charmaine knew their parents would be sitting there.

'Pull up your hood,' she whispered, as they lingered on the threshold of the porch.

They both had hoods on their jumpers. Pulling them well forward, to shield their faces, they dashed across the street and scrambled down the promenade wall as speedily as they could. Now they were out of sight. On the beach. In the dark.

It was a bit like jumping off a cliff. The high promenade behind them was the only fixed point in an otherwise unknown world.

Charmaine and her family had come down to this very

beach every day for the last week, when it was crowded with sand-castle building children, lazing grown-ups, swimmers, boaters, kite-fliers and ice-cream vans.

It was totally different at night. Now, as her eyes adjusted, the distant gurgles of the sea and the twinkling of lights on the headland were the only things which reminded her of the beach's other, daytime self.

Charmaine felt at a loss. What on earth was she doing on the beach, at eleven o'clock at night? The sound of hooves had faded. There was nothing else to remind her of her dream. She looked about in bewilderment, trying to penetrate the blackness.

She was frightened too and very glad she had brought Leon with her. She had a strong sense that they were intruders here.

And then, on the wind, the faint thud of hooves reached her straining ears once more. She pressed her face close to Leon's.

'D'you hear it now?' she whispered urgently.

Leon shook his head. She could tell he was afraid. She stood listening, as the sound got louder and closer.

The pony was unmistakably galloping towards them, from the direction of the headland. Charmaine turned to face him.

She heard Leon gasp beside her. She felt a sense of relief that he could see it too.

'Don't stand there!' cried Leon, tugging at her sleeve. 'The horse might knock you over.'

'He won't,' said Charmaine. She was feeling more and more excited.

'Charmaine!' yelled Leon, as the dark shape came swiftly nearer. She shook herself free from his grasp and stood her ground. From the corner of her eye, Charmaine

saw Leon race back and press himself against the promenade wall. She sniffed in triumph. He'd always been
nervous of horses.

She stood stock still. She knew the pony would stop. It
was still difficult to see him clearly then he loomed before
her – grey as the dark sea. Her dappled grey pony, with
eyes like green salt-smoothed glass.

He scudded to a halt, kicking up puffs of sand, threw up
his head and whinnied.

Charmaine stroked his neck and spoke soothing words
in his ear. He grew still as she summoned all her courage to
mount him.

Seeing the pony standing calmly, Leon ran back down
the sand to join his sister.

'Is he friendly?' he asked, patting the pony gingerly.
'Where's he come from?'

'Give me a leg-up,' Charmaine ordered.

'What!' cried Leon. 'You aren't going to ride him!'

'Of course I am,' said Charmaine. 'What d'you think
I've come down here for?'

'But, but he looks like a wild pony. He'll throw you.
He'll kick you … !'

'Shut up, Leon,' snapped Charmaine. 'You don't know
the first thing about horses. Give me a leg-up. NOW!'

In one agile movement, she was on the pony's back. She
dug her hands into skeins of his long, wiry mane.

Contrary to Leon's prediction, the grey pony didn't try
to buck her off. She looked round. Her brother had
retreated to the safety of the wall.

'See!' she called, laughing. 'He knows me!'

The headlights of a passing car picked out Leon's white
face. He was starting to move back to her, his arm raised.
'Hey!' he shouted. 'You can't go off …' but the rest of his

words failed to reach her ears. The pony had started cantering away.

Charmaine felt that lurch of fear once more as the pony leaped away. She leaned well forward, partly clinging to his neck, gripping his sleek body between her knees.

She felt she had no control over him. He would take her where he wanted to. His speed accelerated. The salt-spray stung her face, and her legs and arms began to ache with the tension of holding on.

But she was riding him! She bathed in a feeling of total exhilaration. It was just like her dream!

The grey pony ran on until he neared a large rock, which jutted across his path. He could easily have run round it, but he didn't veer from his course in the slightest. Charmaine suddenly realised he was going to jump.

It was an amazing leap. Her heart pounded as the grey pony took her soaring through the blackness. When he landed, he swung round violently, almost unseating her.

She clutched at him, trying to keep her balance. Her breath came in small gasps. The pony's unpredictability started to unnerve her.

But once they were thundering back down the beach towards Leon, her confidence returned. Charmaine used the skills she had been taught, to make the pony stop. To her astonishment, he did.

'That was fantastic,' she called to Leon, a dark shape against the lighter wall. 'I can control him now,' she boasted. 'Come up behind me – you'll love it, I promise.'

As Leon stumbled closer, Charmaine could see he'd been crying.

'Whatever's the matter, you silly?' she said.

'Thought he wouldn't bring you back,' sniffed Leon.

'Are you coming up?'

'No,' he said. 'And you've got to get off.'

'You're a *baby*,' she said, the pony skittering under her. 'I don't know why I brought you.'

Leon wiped his eyes with the back of his sleeve and gave her a strange look. 'Will you get off now and come back to the hotel?' A new, pleading note was in his voice.

'I'm enjoying myself!' said Charmaine. 'I want another gallop before I go back. 'Are you sure you don't want to come with me?'

'Positive,' said Leon, stepping nervously out of the way of the prancing hooves. 'Look, you've got to get *off*, Charmaine!' he yelled suddenly at her.

'What on earth are you frightened of?' she said. 'You can see I can stop him if I want to. Wait here for me. I'll take him the other way along the beach.'

She watched Leon, hands in pockets, head hunched in between his shoulders, make his way back to the promenade wall.

'Come on, my beauty,' she said quietly to the pony patting his neck and squeezing him a little with her knees. 'One more gallop.'

As the grey pony sprang away once more, Charmaine remembered the rest of her dream – that hidden part she had always forgotten on waking:–

The grey pony carried her down the beach to the water's edge and then on, on, into the sea.

Rooted to his back, she passed through the shallows to deeper water and yet deeper, leaving just her head and shoulders above the swell. The pony's head was totally submerged, but this didn't stop his furious gallop.

Stinging brine whipped up into her mouth and eyes, taking her breath away. And then the waters closed over her head too, as the grey pony moved relentlessly forward and down into the depths of the ocean.

Why was this the only time she had been able to recall the ending of her dream? Or was her imagination playing tricks on her?

Charmaine looked behind her at the small figure huddled against the wall. She shuddered and told herself not to be so stupid.

She had ridden the pony successfully up and down the beach, hadn't she? She had stopped him when she wanted to, hadn't she? Relaxing once more, she gave herself up to the thrill of the ride.

Although it was so dark, Charmaine quickly became conscious that the pony was no longer moving straight along the beach, but was tracing a wide arc, which was bringing them gradually closer to the sea.

With a sickening lurch, she felt the pony's pace quicken. He was heading straight for the water.

Using all her willpower, she tried to stop his headlong dash.

'Whoah, beauty! That's enough now! Stop, will you, stop!' she yelled.

But her voice seemed to be flung aside by the wind. And the pony did not respond at all.

She tried to calm her mounting terror. This could not really be happening!

As she reached the water's edge, she braced herself to jump from the pony's back. At this speed, she would almost certainly be injured. Better that than drowning!

But as she tried to fling herself off, she found her legs pinioned to the pony. By what force, she could not tell, but she could not move them. They were stuck fast.

Spray-soaked, she stared wide-eyed as the pony careered through the shallows. Even in her terror, she could still register surprise at how long a stretch of shallow water they were passing through.

Then she realised, they were crossing a ridge of sand-banks. Once they reached the edge of these, they would plummet into very deep water.

'Stop!' she shrieked. 'Stop! Stop!'

She could not exert any pressure with her knees. Her legs felt as though they no longer belonged to her. But she yanked hard on the mane hair twined around her fingers.

If anything this only made the pony gallop faster. Charmaine closed her eyes. Her dream had turned into a terrible nightmare. A nightmare from which she might never wake.

Then a higher pitched sound than the sea-roar jolted her.

It was a voice; a thin, pure treble voice. Her brother was singing.

She twisted round and saw him, standing at the water's edge, like a small solitary choir-boy singing a solo at the head of the nave of a great cathedral.

'Leon!' she called. 'Save me!'

He went on with his song, the high notes darting across the expanse of shallow water like fine arrows. She thought she had never heard anything so sad, or so lovely, as his singing.

The grey pony seemed to quiver under her, to the same pulse as the song Leon sang.

Charmaine quivered too and sobbed. The pony was becoming less solid, somehow. It was almost as if she were being carried on a grey cloud.

As the singing speared the air around them, Charmaine felt the grey pony dissolving under her, back into the grey sea-mist from which he came. Until, at last, she stood astride the grey sea-water only, mounding and breaking against her shivering legs.

'You all right?' Leon panted, splashing up alongside her.

The moon came out just then, from behind banks of cloud. Both children saw a ripple moving away across the surface of the deep water ahead.

'That could have been me,' whispered Charmaine. She turned to her brother. They were both crying. Charmaine knew that things had changed between them, and within herself. That other Charmaine had been given her freedom. She no longer felt jealous.

She hugged Leon fiercely. 'Thank you,' she said. 'That singing … !'

'It was the only thing I could think of,' he said simply.

Charmaine took his hand and they headed back in the direction of the hotel lights, together.

fingle hall

angela bull

S top the car,' Mum told Dad. 'Look, darling. There!' She pointed. 'Fingle Hall. Our new home.'

I hadn't seen it before. I'd been ill. Now I peered through the gap between my scarf and hood at Fingle Hall.

Crooked walls; hunched gables; narrow windows squinting through a dense, dark mat of ivy. Sinister! The ivy was the worst thing. It clasped the old house in a smothering embrace, squeezing out life and light.

'It's horrible!' I cried.

Mum and Dad laughed.

'It's romantic,' said Mum.

'And different,' added Dad.

'And haunted,' continued Mum.

'Haunted?' I gulped.

'By the Grey Lady,' Mum explained light-heartedly. 'She's the ghost of a poor girl living here long ago, whose lover was killed in battle. People say she wanders through the house, looking for him.'

'*And you're making me live here?*' I shrieked.

'Don't be such a goose. You'll love it.'

Do *your* parents ever understand you?

Dad and Mum had fallen in love with Fingle Hall. They thought sloping floors and low beams, twisting stairs and huddled rooms, were perfect. I was the scaredy-cat, jumping at a creaking floorboard, a scutter behind the panelling, or the long-nailed scratch of ivy across the windows.

'Cut down the ivy, Dad,' I begged.

But he laughed, and said he couldn't. The ivy held the house together.

Mum and Dad chortled as they tried to straighten pictures on bulging walls, and wedge cupboards that slithered sideways. My nerves jangled like tambourines; my head ached; and I hid myself in bed.

Do you blame me?

So I was alone when I saw her; the Grey Lady. Rain darkened the sky; ivy muffled the window; my bedroom was dim and cold. I pulled the pillows round my ears, and the quilt over my chin, but I dared not shut my eyes. They stared into the gloom –

And suddenly, like a mist, or a swirl of dust motes, she was there, gliding past my bed. Grey, all grey; and transparent as tissue paper. I glimpsed a bowed head, long curls, a cobweb dress that rippled backwards – and then she was gone.

Or not quite gone. I let out my breath, breathed in, sniffed. The room was filled with a sweet fragrance like dried roses, which the Grey Lady had left behind.

Well! It could have been worse. I lay stiff and tense, my nails biting into my palms. I didn't want to see her again. Definitely not! Who'd *want* to see a ghost? Yet, all the same, I felt she wouldn't harm me; she hadn't even noticed me. She was wrapped in her own sorrows, poor, melancholy, rose-scented Lady.

For the next day or two, when I heard creakings and rustlings, I didn't mind so much. Maybe *she* was passing, seeking her lost lover. Maybe she fluttered a fan, or twitched her dress above the dust.

But I still didn't like the ivy. It hissed and nagged, like a fretful voice, across the window panes. Even Mum complained laughingly that it made the rooms dark.

'OK. I'll prune it back on Saturday,' promised Dad.

Before Saturday something good happened. I started at

my new school, and liked my teacher. She was called Mrs Wood, and she was interested to hear I lived at Fingle Hall.

'That fantastic old house!' she exclaimed. 'It must be full of interesting things.'

'Yes,' I agreed – although really it was only full of things belonging to Mum and Dad and me.

'Do bring something along for our Special Display Table,' suggested Mrs Wood.

'Right,' I said, hoping she'd forget.

Teachers do, quite often.

Saturday came, and I was getting out of bed, when I caught a sudden whiff of roses. I glanced round, and there she was again; that grey shape, tissue fine, gliding past me. The misty head drooped, the frail hands hung, the dress fluttered.

I jerked backwards. Maybe she was harmless – yes, she *was* harmless – but she was still a ghost. I didn't like her. If Dad cut the ivy, that might get rid of her.

He began that afternoon. I watched from the window of a corner room, across the landing from my bedroom. Looking down, I could see the top of his head, and his struggle as the tough ivy roots resisted his saw. He grasped an ivy stem, and pulled it. A cloud of dust, grey as the Lady, billowed out of the knotted branches, making him sneeze, and something rattled down from amongst the tangled leaves. Dad bent down to retrieve it.

'Queen Victoria penny,' he called.

I hardly heard, for the ivy tendrils, dragged across the window, were shrieking like voices.

'You mustn't go! You *can't!*'

'Your Mama says I must.'

'When I'm *ill? Dying?*'

My blood ran cold. Whose were these voices? Were

they real? No, of course not, I told myself. They were just ivy leaves, ivy leaves scrawling across glass. That was all.

Dad attacked again. The saw screamed sideways; the first voice screamed too.

'I know Mama's jealous, but I'll *die* if she makes you go. Margery!'

Twigs and leaves showered down. Dad pounced on something else.

'Funny old photo in a frame,' he said. 'Looks like an old-fashioned servant.'

But those other voices were zinging through my head; those ivy-scratch voices. The desperate child, the woman, locked in some old tragedy that I didn't want to know about.

Dad wrenched the ivy stems again. Anguish seared the air.

'– just your name – I'll hide it for ever –'

I hurtled away, down to the garden, like a bat out of hell. Little square objects were still dropping through the ivy. As I reached Dad, he scooped some up.

'Blow me! The things people lose in the ivy! Alphabet bricks.'

He handed me some, and their solidity, against my sweating palms, brought a kind of calm. What could be less ghostly than a small child's brick? Each one had a faded pattern of flowers surrounding a coloured letter.

One displayed an E, another an R.

'Make a word?' challenged Dad, chucking over the rest.

There were seven of them. I spread them on the grass – and suddenly a word sprang out at me. 'GREY.' My heart turned over. Grey Lady? But no. There were only three letters left. R – A – M.

Grey Ram?

'They spell Grey Ram,' I told Dad.

'Very suitable,' Dad replied. He pointed to the field beyond the garden wall, which was full of the frisking lambs of March. 'Plenty of little grey rams there,' he said.

And out in the open air, with the lambs, and the harmless bricks, I was suddenly cool as a daffodil. Maybe the Grey Lady had had a pet lamb. Maybe, like Mary's lamb in the nursery rhyme, it had followed her round the house. I liked the idea. I could almost imagine her, with her flowing curls, and fluttering dress, leading the lamb on a ribbon.

Well out of my sight, of course.

Another thought struck me. The alphabet bricks could be an 'interesting thing' to show Mrs Wood. I wrote 'Grey Ram' with them on the windowsill in the corner room before I went to bed.

There was no scent of roses in my bedroom that night. Instead I caught a whiff of something damp and earthy. Ignoring it, I fell asleep.

I could sleep, then.

There was a surprise when I went to collect the bricks before school on Monday. They'd been changed round on the windowsill. The M was at the beginning now; the Y switched to the end. Mum must have been fiddling with them. I swept them into my bag, without looking too carefully.

'Victorian alphabet bricks! Wonderful!' gushed Mrs Wood.

'They spell "grey ram",' I explained. 'We've got a ghost, called the Grey Lady. I think she must have had a pet sheep.'

I hadn't guessed how sensational this would sound. Excitement flared through the class.

'A ghost! Wow! What's it like?'

'Well –' I couldn't really describe the Grey Lady. 'Scary.'

The class gaped at me, and I felt important. It's nice to feel important when you're new.

'You must arrange the bricks on the Special Display Table, in the hall,' said Mrs Wood. 'Why don't you draw a picture, to go with them?'

I laboured to get it right; the Grey Lady with her long curls, the frisking lamb on its ribbon. Then Andy from Hilltop Farm leaned over me, smelling of muck and straw.

'That's not a ram,' he jeered. 'Rams are great strong brutes, with long horns. Dangerous,' he added.

'Not the Grey Lady's,' I snapped, and I coloured its eyes a charming blue.

Unlike Andy, the Grey Lady at least smelled of roses.

Mum had got home from work just before me. As I opened the front door, she called out, her voice shaky.

'That you, darling? Come to the kitchen. Quick!'

I dashed.

She was standing, white-faced, in a sea of devastation. Someone had ransacked the room, emptying cupboards and drawers all over the floor. Plates and saucepans, spoons and knives, lay tumbled, higgledy-piggledy, among powdery heaps of flour and salt, and shining scatters of currants. Even the fridge door flapped, dripping milk into the chaos.

'Burglars?' I gasped.

'I don't think so. I've done a quick check round, and nothing's been taken. The TV, the video, my rings – they're all here.'

'Then what – ?'

'I don't know. Maybe someone looking for food.'

Her voice quivered.

'Well, not the Grey Lady. She can't eat,' I said, trying, with a joke, to coax a smile from Mum's scared face. I was scared too, but the worst thing was Mum's terror.

'No.' She did smile, wanly. 'Put the kettle on, love. I'll ring the police.'

As I filled the kettle, I noticed the smell. Not curry powder, or mustard, or orange juice, though these bespattered the floor. It was the dark, dank stench of wet earth.

'Can you smell it?' I asked Mum, when she returned.

She sniffed.

'M'm. Only it can't be anything to do with this mess. Probably Dad stirred up the soil when he was pruning the ivy.'

The police were as baffled by the kitchen as we were. There was no evidence of a break-in. The locks were secure, and there were no smashed windows. We cleared up, and I went to bed early, but I couldn't sleep. Even though I didn't like her, I half longed for the Grey Lady's fragrance, to quell the earthy stink which hung round.

Longed? For a ghost?

I got away as quickly as possible next morning. School was safe, and I didn't want to think about Fingle Hall.

I arrived home that afternoon, quaking with dread, but Mum was drinking tea and watching television.

'No more trouble. The kitchen's fine,' she said. 'I don't think we'll ever solve the mystery, so we may as well forget it.'

I tried to, but the house seemed tense with – something. Creaking, rattling. Was it the Grey Lady? Bedtime came, I climbed reluctantly upstairs, and that smell hit me again.

It filled the landing; sour, dense, threatening. All at once, I couldn't breathe for it. I flung open the nearest door, to get some air. It was the corner room, from which I'd watched Dad, and, as I saw it, my heart plummeted.

There was chaos, total chaos, just as there'd been in the kitchen. Drawers had been pulled out, and turned upside down, in some frantic search. The carpet was shoved back, pictures ripped down, and the window gaped wide, letting in that graveyard stink.

Graveyard? Why did I think that? For I was certain of one thing. The Grey Lady would never behave so madly.

Holding my breath, I leaped to the window, and slammed it shut. The ivy screeched along the glass.

'Who's taken – ?'

I nearly blanked out. Somehow I stumbled across the landing, and fell on to my bed, shaking. I wasn't brave enough to face the dark stairs, and tell Mum and Dad. I might meet – what?

I felt oddly guilty too, as if the disorder was my fault.

But I hadn't done anything wrong, had I?

I didn't look in the corner room next morning. I hurried away to the safety of school. All day I dreaded what I might find when I got home, but, in fact, everything was peaceful. The TV hummed, Mum and I flipped through a magazine together, Dad studied Scottish holiday brochures.

'Loads of old castles here. Wonder if they've got ghosts, like us.'

I wished he wouldn't say such things. I hated our ghost.

Ghosts?

I went slowly upstairs at bedtime. The floorboards creaked and snapped under my feet, but, for a moment, the smell was fainter. Daringly, I peeped into the corner room. Yuk! The window was open again; the earth stink streamed in. Slamming the door, I flew to my bedroom, but the smell billowed after me, like a dark wave; choking, overpowering, bitter as death.

There was a crash. I spun round. My dressing-table mirror reflected the landing through my open door, and I saw, with horror, that the corner room door had burst open again. Could it be – oh, let it be! – just a draught from the open window, blowing it wide.

No. There was something there; a blur, transparent in the gloom. Not the Grey Lady. I strained my eyes, and made out a shape – a girl, skeleton thin, stiff and upright, her mouth a dark hole, gaping to shriek.

'*Margery!*'

She was as white as death, as frail as tissue paper. Through the torn and mudstained nightdress she was wearing, I could see the solid door frame. Against it, her face was needle sharp; her black hair, wet and bedraggled. Her hollow, black-ringed eyes glared; her bony hands twisted together.

She paused, then darted straight into my room. I tried to cry out, but the scream caught in my throat, blocked by her graveyard smirch. She didn't look at me. She flew to my dressing-table, tugging out the drawers, and hurling their contents on the floor in a manic search.

'Where are they?' she cried angrily; springing, weightless, towards the wardrobe, burrowing, snatching.

Foiled again, she threw open the window. Her ghostly hands scrabbled in the ivy, dragging its tendrils across the pane to mingle with her cries.

'They've gone! Oh Margery! I meant to save them –'

And, at last, I understood. My voice, loud with terror, broke through hers.

'I'll bring back the bricks tomorrow.'

She flashed round, stared. Then suddenly the room was empty; empty, free – except for the dank, dead smell of her shroud.

For it wasn't a nightdress she was wearing. It was a shroud, stained with the earth of her burial.

I cowered on my bed, panting and trembling. Here was no gentle Grey Lady, seeking her lover. This ghost had climbed out of her grave, to scour the house for her alphabet bricks. Because they spelled –

Not Grey Ram.

I suddenly remembered the old framed photo, hidden in the ivy too.

Gathering my courage, I crept downstairs. Dad had left the picture on the hall table. I picked it up, and looked at it properly for the first time.

It showed the round, cheery face of a young woman, in a servant's uniform. The eyes were kind, the mouth smiled, the hair was tucked tidily under a cap. She wore a pinafore over a plain dress.

You'd have been glad if she'd looked after you when you were ill.

But Mama had been jealous of her; jealous because the sick child loved her kind nursemaid more than her harsh mother. So the nursemaid was sent away, and the child had died of a broken heart without her. But, before she'd died, she'd hidden a secret talisman in the ivy – the nursemaid's name, spelled out in alphabet bricks. Being near, it had perhaps brought her comfort.

I slid my fingernail into the crack round the frame, and prised it open. The photo slid out. I turned it over, and saw a name, written in childish capitals on the back.

MARGERY.

As I gazed, the letters seemed to rearrange themselves.

GREY RAM.

If I'd looked properly at the bricks on the windowsill, two days ago, when they'd been set in order by ghostly hands, they'd have given me Margery's name.

Back in bed, I lay stiffly alert, waiting in case the ghost came back. But she didn't, though I stayed awake all night. It was something to know she'd believed my promise.

Willpower alone got me to school next day.

'Can I take back my bricks?' I croaked to Mrs Wood. 'Somebody needs them.'

'Yes, of course. Goodness!' she stared at me. 'You look awful. Are you all right? Has anyone upset you?'

Just a ghost, I wanted to answer; a desperate, searching ghost.

But I didn't say a word.

I hurried to be home from school before Mum got back. I dashed upstairs, threw open the window of the corner room, and plunged the bricks and the photo in the ivy, as deeply as I could.

'There!' I shouted. 'You can have them back. I'm sorry I took them. They'll be safe now. So please, *please*, don't search any more.'

Out on the landing again, my legs gave way. Shattered, I sank on to the dipping floorboards.

All at once, I caught a faint fragrance of roses. The Grey Lady drifted past me, curls drooping, dress rippling gently behind her.

I sighed with strange relief. She seemed so familiar, so *safe*.

Daft as it may seem, I *liked* the Grey Lady.

flute

marjorie darke

The eyes hung in the darkness.

I'm not joking! They were really there – in front of my drawn curtains. No body. No face. Just two glowing golden eyes. Creepy!

I'd gone to bed early because next day was our Swimming Gala. We mean to win the House Trophy for the sixth time, and I'm down to swim two lengths breaststroke for our house – Symes that is. We have four houses in our school – all named after VIPs. Georgie told me that old Symes was the mayor of our town ages ago, and he built our housing estate, and something else I didn't catch because I dropped a jam-jar of tadpoles I was carrying … *panic!*

Anyway, VIPs weren't important now. I stared back at the eyes seeing little flecks of green around the dark holes of their pupils, and goosebumps came out all up my arms. Even my warm duvet didn't stop the shivers. I wanted to hide, or switch on the bedside lamp … anything to break from that golden gaze – but all I did was act like a bit of jelly.

'Don't be a rabbit, Gemma,' my mind said. 'Eyes must belong to a face. Turn on the light. Find out!'

But somehow my hand seemed to have lost its bones and muscles. At last Nature took over, making me blink.

Down, up.

In that flick, the eyes vanished. I tried another blink to make sure.

Down, up.

Still no eyes.

Now I did switch on the light.

Instant cheerfulness! Red walls, white curtains, posters

of The Sandblasters, Jason Maynard, my Emperor penguins. Jeans, sweater, knickers, socks in a heap on the sunflower rug. My Walkman and tapes, unfinished homework sprawled over my table. Nothing remotely like floating eyes.

Well, that was that. But to be on the safe side I kept the light on, and dropped into a sleep full of uncomfortable dreams.

Next morning, it wasn't bad dreams that woke me, but Louise doing her flute practise. Louise is my sister, she's twelve – two years older than me – and she's going in for her grade four exam next week. I remember thinking 'Not a hope if she plays like that'! Then I saw the clock – *five past eight*! I fell out of bed. Hunted for my swimsuit, grabbed toast and apple juice at a run, flung homework into my bag.

'Don't forget your sandwich box.' Mum pressed it into my hand. 'Good luck with the swimming. Have you got your goggles?'

Goggles! I'd forgotten all about them, but it was after half past eight now. I'd have to sprint if I wasn't to miss the bus.

'Yes,' I lied and shot outdoors, racing to the bus stop – arriving just as the bus drew up.

Georgie was there, waiting.

'Hi!' She pushed her specs back up her nose. 'You've dropped your goggles.'

I glanced down. They were in the gutter. Mine all right – GEMMA FIELDING written in big red letters along one strap. I couldn't think how they had got there and was squatting to pick them up, when two things happened.

First the driver got snotty: 'Are you getting on this bus or not?'

Then, as I grabbed the goggles, a weird electric shock fizzed through my hand, making me let go.

He revved his engine. 'Can't wait all day!'

Gingerly, with buzzing fingertips, I picked up the goggles, and dropped them into my bag. When we were in our seats, I told Georgie.

'You mean like stripping off a sweater and making sparks, or brushing your hair and it crackles and stands on end?' with another shove at her specs.

I nodded.

'Static. Sure to be. Happens in hot weather as well as cold, hadn't you noticed?'

'Okay, but that doesn't explain how they came to be in the gutter in the first place.'

'Fell out of your pocket. How else?'

Georgie has answers for everything, so I decided to try her with the eyes.

'Overworked imagination, Gem. You sweated about the Swimming Gala and had a nightmare.'

'I didn't! They were *there* I tell you.'

'Bouncing about on bits of elastic in the middle of the night I suppose?'

'Oh yeah and you were in my bedroom, were you?' I snapped.

'Keep your hair on. If *I'd* have told *you* this eye thing, wouldn't you have said "a nightmare"?'

I muttered: 'Didn't imagine it. No way …' I might have gone on but, as the bus started again, Brian Millerchip came lurching along the aisle grinning all over his stupid face.

'If it isn't the Gee-Gees!' He began to make clopping noises as if we were a couple of ponies. His idea of a joke but he never gives it a rest.

'Think you're so clever!' I said. 'Buzz off!' I can't stand him with his greasy hair-do and jeans at half mast.

'Oh sorry your Majesty – forgot you're the Gala Queen!' He went on down the aisle, arms flailing and feeble swimming noises coming out of his sloppy mouth.

'Take no notice,' Georgie said as we got off the bus and into the hot July sunshine. 'He's only jealous because you can swim better than him … and he fancies you.'

'*Georgina!*'

The things she says!

Our school swimming bath is primitive, so any Gala takes place in the local Leisure Centre, which has three pools – Learners, Main pool and a separate diving pit. It's a great place – air-conditioned and super clean, with goodies like showers and hair-dryers and foot-baths. So long as you behave everything is fine, but start horsing about and you are out, full stop. Water games with blown up rings or balls are only allowed in the Learners, and of course pets are absolutely forbidden anywhere.

Jumpy Jarman, our P.E. teacher, was giving last minute tips. 'Don't forget to pace yourselves. Remember not to start too fast … keep an easy rhythm. Good luck every-one!'

Georgie waved from the stand as I took my place on the edge of the bath. The way the scoring was going, the trophy depended on this last race … on *me!* I put on my goggles. My stomach was tying itself in knots. I'm always twitchy before any competition, but today was extra bad. How I was going to swim, I couldn't imagine!

An announcement was made about the race. We got the signal:

'On your marks!'

Then the starter gun fired.

Usually, as I dive into the water, fright disappears. But today I got the angle wrong and hit the surface hard, almost knocking the breath out of me as the others steamed away down their lanes. Inside my head I was swearing and trying not to because it didn't help Jumpy's 'easy rhythm'. I was way behind and really upset – so when I came up for air and found those Golden Eyes looking straight at me, I nearly died!

Mega-terror!

Instinct bellowed SWIM FOR THE SIDE – but, strangely, I *could not*. The Eyes pulled me forward, like a magnet, all the time moving away. I kept thinking – swim past … swim past … But no matter how I tried, the distance between us didn't shrink. It was like one of those awful nightmares. Without doubt they were the same golden eyes I'd seen last night – green flecks; pupils like dark holes.

Nothing made sense.

First length finished. I turned. Came up for air. Golden Eyes was still there. By now I was desperate to get away and shot off like a bullet from a gun, swimming for my life.

Half a length to go. This was a mega-fast swim, but I kept waiting for the race to be stopped. Someone *must* notice what was going on?

Nothing happened. All around, splashing and shouts. In and out of the water went my arms, my head. Slowly, surely, I closed on the others, and my panic eased a fraction as it dawned that the Eyes were acting like a pace-maker. Us together – a strange team.

I touched the end of the bath, and heard cheers as my head came out of the water, but took a second to realise I had won. I could hardly believe my luck and snatched off my goggles whirling them in the air, thrilled. The trophy was ours! Terrific! I glanced round to check on the Eyes, but couldn't see them and a sudden thought hit me – was it the *goggles* playing tricks? Hastily I put them on again and looked down the pool. Behind the heads of the last swimmers, the water rippled and churned emptily.

'Did you see?' I asked Georgie when I reached the cubicle and was towelling myself.

'What?' She had sneaked down from the stand to bring me a Mars Bar and held it out. 'Prize for being first.'

I said: 'Thanks … well did you?'

'Did I what?'

'See those golden eyes, dopey. They were in front of me the whole time – pulling me on.'

Georgie looked worried. 'Eat up that Mars Bar quick, Gem. Your bloodsugar count must be very low. You're hallucinating.'

When she's stirred up, Georgie lets out loads of scientific slop.

I nearly argued, but knew I'd be on a loser. Undoing the Mars Bar I took a mouthful of chocolate instead.

That was on Friday and over most of the weekend nothing weird happened. It was hot, and I mooched about in shorts and a sun top while Louise spent a lot of time practising so badly, I asked her at Sunday breakfast what was wrong.

'Nothing. What are you on about?' She emptied most of the marmalade jar on her piece of toast.

'The notes keep splitting – like as if two flutes are playing tunes that don't match … hey, leave some for me!'

'You've got waxy ears. My flute playing is brilliant.' She took another piece of toast and scraped the last of the marmalade over it. 'I shall get a distinction!'

I made a grab for her toast, knocking it sticky side down on the floor.

'Behaving like infants!' Dad said, coming in with the teapot in one hand and Sunday papers in the other.

'Wasn't me,' Louise said smugly.

I could have hit her.

Upstairs I stuck on one of my favourite tapes and flopped on the floor with my feet propped against the wardrobe.

Next thing, Louise had started up her playing again, louder and worse than ever. I could hear it even with my headphones on. She was deliberately trying to annoy me, *I knew*, and I stormed out of my room and into hers. No Louise, but her instrument was in its open case on her dressing table. Flute sounds drifted up the stairs. Following them down, I went out of the front door.

There, on our path, sat a dog – forehead wrinkled, mouth open letting out this weird fluting noise! That was peculiar enough, but then I saw its eyes. *Golden eyes.* I couldn't move.

Seeing me, it shut up and came closer, curled tail twitching. It didn't look at all threatening, but my neck prickled and my brain reeled with the effort of trying to connect the Before with the Now and getting nowhere.

'Hi, Flute!' I said nervously, feeling my palms go sticky. 'Hey, that's the right name for you isn't it, boy?'

By this time his whole bum was wagging – very friendly, so I braved it and rubbed between his ears. But instead of meeting a hard furry head, an electric shock fizzed up my arm as my hand *went in!* I leapt back, trembling, and might have sprinted indoors if Flute hadn't come and sat at my feet, head cocked, eyes all hopeful, offering a paw. He was so sweet! Part of me wanted to take it, but I didn't fancy another shock.

We looked at each other. Then his nose pushed at my bare knee – not the usual damp dog-nose feel, but a strong shivery tickle, as if an outsize spider had landed by mistake and was scuttling off.

That's when Mum opened the door. 'There you are! I've been looking everywhere. Nip to the corner shop and get a pint of milk, Gemma. We've run out.'

No mention of the dog, though Flute was as large and *there* as ever.

'Everything look okay to you?' I asked casually, taking the money.

She was surprised. 'Yes. Why, is something wrong?'

'No ... no nothing. Shan't be long.' I scooted out of the gate, Flute galloping after me, pink tongue flopping.

Down the road we went, passing several people I know. They all said 'Hello!' but nothing about the dog.

Outside the shop I told Flute to 'Stay', leaving him sitting on the pavement, or so I thought – until I met him coming round the end of the shelves of magazines. I was about to tick him off, when Mrs Harrington our neighbour, who was buying newspapers, saw me.

'Hello, Gemma! I'll wait and we can walk back together.'

She went out and I collected milk from the cool-cupboard and paid, while Flute wandered about, nobody noticing. We walked home, Mrs H chatting on about Louise's flute exam and how the hedge between our gardens needed cutting – boring stuff. Not a word about my Flute though he was trotting beside me. Only when we got to our gates and he dashed straight through her sideways, did she give a big shiver and said:

'Somebody must have walked over my grave!'

That's how it went on for the rest of Sunday. Everywhere I went Flute came with me ... even to the loo!

When I went to get a glass of squash he almost climbed into the fridge. Then the berk dodged right through me as I was going into the living-room to watch *Neighbours*. I learned exactly what Mrs H meant about someone walking over her grave. Shuddery! I dropped my squash.

'Oh Gemma!' Mum fetched a cloth.

As if that wasn't bad enough, Flute didn't lie down, but pushed his head right into the screen, making a snow-storm – the sound turning to a swarm of angry bees.

'Flute!' I shouted,

'Don't blame Louise,' Mum fiddled with the controls. 'Her flute can't possibly affect the telly … what's the matter with you two anyway, scrapping all day …'

It was time to be somewhere else. 'I'm going to have a bath,' I said.

But Flute got there first, and when I was in and sloshing around with the sponge, he put his paws on the edge, gazing at the water. I thought he was going to jump in and join me … but he didn't.

Monday morning on the bus I kept quiet, trying not to touch Flute who lay under the seat. But when we reached the cloakroom, I couldn't hold back any longer and told Georgie about Flute's doings over the weekend.

At first she scoffed: 'Your imagination is working overtime.' Opening her locker she chucked in her sports gear, and slammed the door shut.

'Flute's in your locker,' I told her, then as his nose poked through the metal: 'Don't worry, he's coming out.'

'I suppose there is a baboon and a giraffe as well!' She marched off down the corridor.

I hurried after her. 'Just a dog. And I'm not making it up!' But she wouldn't listen.

Kids were milling about, and Flute was dashing up and

down in the most hairy way. Luckily he didn't go through anyone.

We had Assembly – Flute joining in the hymn making the most awful racket.

In maths – first lesson – Flute got bored, put his paws on my knees and started licking my face. I could help letting out a squeak with all that electricity fizzing about – and Ms Pattimore told me off for being silly, and kept me behind at the end of the lesson. She moaned on and on about the importance of paying attention, while Flute kept pushing at me with his nose which made me hop about. At last Ms Pattimore got really snotty.

'You aren't listening to a word I say, Gemma. We shall see what a detention will do!'

So there I was with a detention and a dog nobody could see and break was over and the day threatening to go from bad to worse.

In English things got really out of hand. When we were supposed to be writing a description of 'My Best Friend', Flute jumped on the table and put his paws on my exercise book. There wasn't a thing I could do. I couldn't push him away because of the electricity fizz. I couldn't order him to get down because everyone would think I'd gone bonkers.

His paws were very neat, smooth and brown with little black nails. I began to draw round them, taking care my biro didn't touch a single hair.

'So – your best friend is a dog is it, Gemma?'

I jumped. Mr Hall was standing over me. He tapped my exercise book with his finger. 'Unfortunately this isn't an art class. Words are what we need, not pawprints. My Best Friend,' another tap of his finger. 'Describe your dog – what does he look like, the tricks he gets up to … that sort of thing but *in words*.' He glanced at his watch. 'Listen everyone – I want this work completed by tomorrow, so finish off as homework.'

And I hadn't written a single word!

'What *were* you doing?' Georgie asked as we went to get our lunch.

'It was Flute's fault,' I began but she interrupted.

'Might have known you'd blame the ghost dog!'

'He's not a ghost. Ghosts are all sheety with cutout black eyeholes, or else people in old-fashioned clothes carrying their heads under their arms. Watch my mouth – *This Is A Dog.*'

For once she didn't have any smart answers.

The afternoon turned out worse than the morning. Athletics on the games field – and didn't Flute love it! We were practising for Sports Day, and he tore along the track when we did our sprints, sprang over the high bar, and went like a rocket for the sand pit where we do long-jump. Half crazy with excitement he went through kids as if they were thin mist, making them trip up, fall over each other, catch their toes on the high bar.

Jumpy Jarman was doing her nut – she's a real shouter when she gets angry, which to be fair isn't often. The crunch came when to my horror I saw Flute in the long-jump sand digging a hole!

'FLUTE, you berk ... *stop it!*' I ran at him, crashing into Georgie mid air, just as she took off.

We fell in a heap on top of Flute who didn't mind one bit, climbing through us, silly tail twitching. Georgie let out the most almighty shriek and Jumpy came running.

'Georgina, are you all right? Whatever possessed you, Gemma?' She hauled me to my feet.

I could have said: 'A dog,' but would have got an earful for cheek, so didn't. That made her more furious than ever. Kids had strolled over to see what was going on and after making sure Georgie had no broken bones she sent everyone packing. She gave me a detention, adding darkly:

'See me first thing in the morning!'

What a day!

Georgie avoided me when it was time to go home and I went out of the school gates alone – well almost, Flute was there. I didn't rush for the bus. Walking would give me time to think. There was a lot to sort out – mostly, what was I going to do about Flute? I had almost reached the end of the street when someone came up behind.

'Is that your dog,' Brian Millerchip asked.

I was just about to say something cutting when I realised *he was seeing Flute!* My heart did a jig, but I kept my cool.

'What dog?'

'That dog,' he pointed at Flute. 'Is he yours?'

'Not exactly. He keeps following me around. I call him Flute because of this weird noise he makes.'

'Like this?' He made a fair imitation of the sound and next thing, Flute came galloping back. Brian's smirk changed to shock, then to doubt, then became a shaky grin of joy.

'Hi, Bernie old boy … I can't believe this!' he crouched down.

I almost shouted: 'Don't touch him!' but too late.

'Hell!' He collapsed on the pavement, flicking his hand hard.

'Electric shock?' I asked, and when he nodded: 'It's happened to me several times. What did you call him?'

'Bernie – short for Bernado Symes Brownmaster the Third – he's a Basenji, an African hunting dog … Crufts champion,' he scrambled to his feet. 'They can't bark. They yodel. He was my Great-Grandad's prize dog.'

'Was?' I asked.

Brian made a gulping noise. 'Bernie got killed.'

We stared at each other.

'How?' I asked.

He shook his head. I could see he was upset but I had to know. 'Tell me!'

'Took him for a walk, didn't I ... wasn't supposed to ... I was only a little kid, about six ... he tugged like mad ... couldn't hold him ... car came whizzing ...' Mouth tight, Brian stared at Flute.

I was beginning to make connections. 'Your Great-Grandad's name was Symes?'

He nodded again.

'Symes House, Symes?'

'Yes – want to make something of it?' he scowled, but for once instead of being irritated, I felt sorry for him. I had a sudden inspiration.

'Take Bernie home now, why don't you? Call him like before.' We were near where Brian catches the morning bus. 'Go on, try!'

He yodelled. Flute's ears pricked and he dashed up. A big grin spread across Brian's face. He gave me a sideways look.

'Sure you don't mind?'

I knew he meant giving up Flute. Mostly it would be a HUGE relief. And yet I'd grown sort of fond of the dog. After all, he had helped me win the trophy.

Then it dawned ...

'See you both tomorrow!' I said – and crossed the road comfortably alone.

ghost trains

john west

Nick sat bolt upright in bed. He'd heard a noise. He was sure of it. He reached under the bed for his baseball bat, then crept across his room to the open door.

'Who's that?' he shouted.

His voice echoed round the dark empty house. But then he heard it again. That was it, a sort of rumbling, drumming noise. Where was it coming from, inside or outside? There it was again, up above, in the attic.

Nick took a deep shaky breath. It was the first night that he had been left alone in the house. Mum and Dad had gone to see Gran because she had been rushed into hospital and of course Sophie had gone too. There'd been quite a row because Mum had said he couldn't stay on his own, but it was the big game tomorrow, and he was captain.

'I am thirteen, for heaven's sake,' he'd argued.

'Yes, let him stay,' Dad had agreed, 'there's got to be a first time. I'll make sure Bob's home this weekend.'

'Well, I'm still not happy,' said Mum, 'but if you promise to ring Uncle Bob if there's any problem, I suppose ...'

Now Nick stood shaking in his bedroom doorway. He heard the noise again, right above his head.

'There's nothing in the attic except a few old cases and cardboard boxes, Christmas decorations, things like that,' he thought. 'And Grandpa's railway.'

When Granny died – that's the other one, not the one who was ill at the moment – Grandpa Bill had moved into a special flat, and it was too small for the trains. He'd asked

Nick to look after them. But trains don't run on their own, in the middle of the night.

'Some people would hide their valuables in the attic,' he said to himself. 'If a burglar …'

'Now, Nicholas, remember,' Mum had said, 'Uncle Bob is home all weekend and you're to phone him at once if you have any worries.' Mum only called him Nicholas when she was being very serious.

'Yes, Mum, of course.' He hadn't pointed out that she had already told him twice.

So now, should he telephone? He looked at his watch; it was nearly one a.m. He could hardly ring at this hour to say Grandpa's trains were running, on their own.

He edged out onto the landing, clutching the baseball bat tightly. Now there was a noise from downstairs as well, a faint grunting and groaning.

He crept to the top of the stairs and forgot about the one squeaky floorboard. The downstairs noise stopped at once. He waited, then trod on it again to see if that made any difference. It did. There was a loud bark.

'You total idiot,' he said to himself. He had forgotten Ben, who slept in the kitchen. Ben had been snoring, as usual.

Nick leapt down the stairs three at a time and flung open the kitchen door. Ben wagged his tail and licked Nick's hand.

He had to pluck up courage to go back upstairs. Ben sat by the bottom stair, watching. He knew he was not allowed any further. At the top, Nick stopped and listened. Nothing. Not a sound. He knew that, if he went back to bed, he would never get back to sleep. He had to look in the attic.

'Shoes,' he thought and then wondered why. He went quickly back to his bedroom and put on some trainers.

'The attic floor is a bit splintery, but if there's a burglar up there …' He tried to laugh at himself but couldn't.

He hadn't heard the drumming noise for a little while. He opened the door to the attic stairs. It used to be a cupboard. When the trains were moved in, they'd had a sort of conversion done so that Grandpa wouldn't have to climb a ladder. He started up the steep new stairs, very slowly, making a lot of noise, on purpose.

The light switch for the attic was at the top. He switched on and looked round.

Everything seemed normal enough. But then he realised that, before he'd put the light on, it had not been totally black. Bravely, he switched it off again. There was a glow from some of the railway coaches. Grandpa had put little lights in some of them, but surely the electrics could not have been left on.

He could feel a draught. They had put in one of those special attic windows. He walked slowly across to it; it was not properly shut. He opened it wide to slam it. Immediately, the cupboard door at the bottom of the new stairs slammed shut.

'Damn and blast and words I'm not allowed to use,' he said to himself. In the dark he struggled back to the top of the stairs to find the light switch. Good, now back down …

'Oh, no, I don't believe it!' He was now talking out loud. He cursed again.

'You must remind me, dear,' Dad had said, umpteen times, 'about that cupboard door.'

'Yes,' Mum had replied, 'we don't want Grandpa to be stuck up there.'

Being a cupboard door, it had never had a handle on the inside. It still did not have a handle on the inside. He was stuck, locked in. He heard the drumming noise again from above.

'Ben, Ben,' he screamed. 'Come up here.'

But Ben was far too well trained. He knew he wasn't allowed upstairs. He just barked loudly instead.

Shaking like a leaf, Nick went back up into the attic. Silence, but then … he couldn't believe his eyes. Two minutes ago the new Intercity 125 had been in the main station; it was now waiting by a stop light the other side of the layout. As he watched, horrified, the little light turned green and the train started forward. A tank engine moved in the goods yard. He threw himself back to the top of the stairs.

The electrician had insisted they must have an extra mains switch for safety. Nick grabbed it and switched off. The trains stopped; the drumming noise they made stopped too. But of course the attic light went out as well. The only sound seemed to be his teeth chattering. He sat down on the floor. It was pitch black. He wanted to cry.

He tried to get his brain in gear. The family were not due back till the next night. Mum and Uncle Bob would phone in the morning to check he was all right and they'd go mad if they didn't get a reply. He was locked in and he couldn't use the electricity because there was a ghost in the works.

He was suddenly conscious of something else, there was no lavatory in the attic. He could probably wait a little while, but the more he thought about it, the more he knew he couldn't wait long.

He edged his way over to the window and looked out. He felt like breaking it; it was the stupid window which had made the door slam. It was too dark to have any idea how far down it would be.

'Don't be totally mad,' he said to himself. 'You cannot jump!'

Then he remembered something, the bits which belonged to Dad's boat. There was a lot of stuff in the attic during the winter.

He inched his way over in the dark to where it would be and started to feel around. There was a slight smell of sea and salt and fishy things. His hands got tangled in a net. Then his fingers closed around some rope. It didn't seem very thick but it was the nylon sort and should be strong enough. But could it be long enough?

He kept pulling at it gently; he didn't want a tangle. He came to another end.

'Damn, not enough.'

He searched and found another piece. In the background, he could hear Ben whining; the poor dog must know something was badly wrong.

Eventually, Nick dragged three reasonable lengths of rope back to the window. There was just enough light to be able to sort out the ends and start knotting. He'd never been a boy scout but Dad had taught him reef knots and things on the boat.

Above the window there was a beam, one of the ones which held the roof up. Nick tied one end of the rope round it, pulled it tight then hung on it with all his weight. It tightened up and seemed quite strong enough. He threw the other end out of the window; the rope snaked down into the darkness.

He climbed up and sat on the window-sill. That was when the shakes came back.

'What are you doing?' he asked himself. 'Have you gone quite mad? You cannot climb down that; you don't even know if it'll reach the ground.'

'Right,' his other self replied, 'and if I don't?'

The argument didn't last long. He couldn't spend the rest of the night shut up alone in the attic, and he was shaking with cold as well as fear. It was now or never.

He tried to remember exactly how they climbed up and down ropes in the gym at school. This was just the same really, he tried to kid himself. He gripped his feet tightly round the rope and gently pushed off from the ledge.

Below the attic window, there was a bit of sloping roof. That was easy. As he came to the edge of the roof, his pyjama trousers caught on the gutter. He tugged at them; they tore. Stupidly he started to worry about what to tell Mum.

'There's no way I'm ever going to tell her about this,' he thought.

The family always thought he was a bit mad but this would give both Mum and Dad heart attacks.

He was now going down vertically, hand over hand, feet still gripping tight. So far, so good. It was bitterly cold. He went past one of the knots in the rope. There was a window nearby but out of reach; that would be Sophie's room. He came to the next knot; now he was on the last piece of rope, with no idea how far down he still had to go.

He started to say some prayers. Unfortunately they didn't seem to work. Suddenly, without any warning, his feet slipped off the end of the rope. How far down could it be? His arms were really starting to hurt.

He tried to remember the layout below Sophie's window but his brain wouldn't work.

'If I drop something,' he said to himself, 'I could listen to how long it took and what it landed on. But I've nothing to drop.'

Except a shoe! He kicked off one trainer with the other foot.

It dropped, crash, breaking glass.

'Oh no, the conservatory, Dad'll kill me'.

Dad had put up a sort of DIY greenhouse, which the family all called the conservatory as a joke. Now it was going to need a repair job, quite a big one if he fell straight through it.

Ben was barking furiously. Poor dog, he must be wondering what on earth is going on.

'But wait, maybe …'

He lowered himself slowly, his arms really killing him. Yes, his feet touched something solid. The top of the greenhouse had a wood frame screwed to the side of the house. He was able to take some weight off his arms.

Still holding firm to the rope, he inched his way sideways. This was the moment when he realised that, even if he reached the ground in one piece, he was locked out. He badly wanted to cry, and he wanted to go to the lavatory even worse.

He had guessed right. His toes felt the corner of the frame, the edge of the greenhouse.

'Okay, go for it,' he said to himself, and jumped to one side. It could have been much worse. He landed in a big bush; it was probably one of Mum's most special ones. Nothing seemed to be broken, although his foot, the one without a shoe on, was hurting. He sat in the bush and wondered what to do next.

'Could I go and wake the neighbours?'

Now that he was safely at ground level, he was still hoping to get away with it, in other words not tell Mum and Dad.

'Wuff,' barked a happy Ben, who had just shot round the corner. Although he must have been quite puzzled by the events of the last half-hour, he was obviously relieved to find Nick.

'Clever boy,' said Nick and gave him a big cuddle. 'I'd forgotten about your doggy flap.'

So that Ben could go out in the garden during the day, when the family were all out at school and work, Dad had fitted a dog-flap into the back door.

'What do you think, old boy? Could I make it? Am I too big?'

They both went round to the door. The hole with the flap looked barely big enough for Ben to get through, let alone Nick.

Perhaps it was inevitable but it was starting to rain. That reminded him of something else he needed to do. He went behind a hedge, which was not really necessary; there was certainly nobody there to watch. Ben got the same idea and went to his favourite tree.

'Now,' Nick said, 'let's try the impossible.'

He got down on hands and knees and put his head through the flap. The kitchen smelt nice and warm. Ben thought this was a game and tried to join in.

'Go away, you silly boy,' said Nick. Ben looked quite hurt.

It was useless. Nick was very big for a thirteen-year-old and could not begin to get his shoulders into the gap. He thought of pulling the whole flap-frame out of the door but he didn't have any tools.

It was not fair, to have been through so much and now to be stuck outside in the rain. He was cold, wet and miserable, locked out of his own home, because ghosts had taken over Grandpa's trains.

He walked down the path to the shed where Dad kept the mower and other garden things; there might be some tools in there. And at least he would be under cover. Ben followed slowly.

The door was never locked. Nick opened it. Inside it

....

seemed extra dark. Ben growled; Nick wondered if perhaps Ben could see or hear things that he couldn't, live things. He stepped inside and, immediately screamed.

'Get off, get off,' he cried. He had walked into a mass of spider's web. He could feel it all over his face. He tried to pull it away with his hands but that seemed to make things worse. He went back outside and scrubbed at himself. He tried to stand still, but couldn't stop shivering.

'Where's it gone?' he wondered. 'Or where have they gone? It must take loads of spiders to make that much webby mess.'

What now? He had to get in the shed to find some tools for the dog flap.

Why had Dad not put the inside handle on the attic door? Why had the stupid door slammed?

'I suppose it was my fault,' he thought, 'because I slammed the window shut. No wait, not quite right. It slammed as I opened the window. Why? Because of the draught. But … a draught needs a way in and a way out. Yes. Of course. Because my bedroom window is open.'

For the first time for what seemed ages, he felt happier. Now all he had to find was the ladder and that was no trouble; he knew it was here in the shed. It was one of those fold-up and extend ladders. He'd used it a few weeks ago when Sophie's kite got stuck in a tree. He was sure it was long enough.

But he hated spiders. Then he had a bright idea.

'Go on, Ben, you go first.' He pushed the poor dog into the shed and crawled in after him. The spiders seemed to have gone into hiding. He stood up gingerly and dragged down the ladder.

In very few minutes he was back in his own room. He pushed the ladder away so that it fell noisily back into the garden. Ben yelped and leapt out of the way; he had watched the climb. Nick closed the window.

He went straight back downstairs and met Ben coming in through the flap. He tried to clean himself up a bit in the kitchen, but all he wanted to do was get back into bed.

He didn't really want to be on his own any more. He tried hard to persuade Ben to come upstairs.

'It's all right, old boy, I promise. I won't tell them.' Nick had to carry him up and then dropped him on the bed; Ben looked bedraggled and very unhappy.

Nick realised that his pyjamas were sopping wet from the rain. He spread them out on the radiator and crawled into bed. He soon felt Ben jump off and heard him curl up on the floor, just by the bed.

When he woke up, he looked at his watch. It was just after eight. Ben was lying on the floor.

'What on earth are you doing up here?' Nick asked him.

It all started to come back. On the radiator were his pyjamas. He looked under the bedclothes; he had nothing on. He got out of bed and picked up the pyjama trousers; there was a bad tear at the bottom of the left leg. It had not been a dream.

The telephone started to ring. He ran into Mum and Dad's room; there was a phone by their bed.

'Hello, this is 1360, who's speaking please?' He could not get out of the habit of answering like Mum had taught him when he was little.

'Hello, dear,' said Mum. 'Sorry to ring so early, but we just wanted to check you were all right.' She laughed. 'We thought you might have been out on the tiles last night.'

Mums use funny expressions sometimes.

'No, no, just fine.' He laughed nervously.

'We've discovered that we can see Gran this morning, so we should be home by about six.'

'Oh, good.' Nick felt he was not being talkative enough.

'I know what you've been doing,' said Mum in a serious voice, 'you stayed up far too late watching television and you were still sound asleep when I rang.'

'Yes, I'm sorry, Mum.' It seemed easier to agree.

'Well, be good, and we'll see you later.'

'Bye, Mum,' and, just in time, he remembered to say, 'and give my love to Gran.'

He wandered back to his bedroom and put on his pyjama trousers. He really wanted to go up in the attic. Could the Intercity have moved again, even without power? He jumped when the telephone rang again.

This time, he just said 'Hello'. It was Grandpa.

'I thought it might be a bit early to ring you but it can't be,' he said. 'When I tried just now, you were engaged.'

'Yes, that was Mum, Grandpa, to see if I was okay.'

'When are you going off to your football?' asked Grandpa.

'About one o'clock,' Nick replied, 'a friend's dad is picking me up.'

'That's good, because I want to come round this morning and finish the computer thing.'

Grandpa was quite a whizz-kid at computers and things. But Nick had no idea what he was talking about.

'You'll have to explain,' he said.

'Oh heavens, surely your father told you. I've rigged up a connection between some new software on his computer and the railway upstairs.'

There was a pause; Nick couldn't think of anything to say.

'Yes,' Grandpa went on, 'it'll mean we can run a whole sequence of train movements automatically. Everything will be covered, the trains of course, and the points, the signals, the lot. And the coach lights will only come on when a train is in use. I almost finished it all yesterday while you were at school.'

Nick felt his brain was beginning to hurt; the pieces of the jigsaw were falling into place.

'Actually, I'm cross with him for not telling you,' Grandpa said. 'It is important, because, until I've finished, it's vital not to turn off that mains switch in the attic. If you do, I'll lose the lot, all the programming I've done. Still, you've probably been stuck in front of the telly, probably haven't even been up there.'

Any words that Nick thought of got stuck in his throat. Grandpa was one of his most favourite people. All he managed to say was 'Bye, Grandpa, see you later.'

Nick sat down on the carpet by his parents' bed. At last, he burst into floods of tears. Ben wandered in and sat next to him. He still looked a bit puzzled.

dolphin story collections

chosen by **wendy cooling**